The
Christmas
Gift

SHIRLEY E. HART

Paperback-Press
an imprint of A & S Publishing
A & S Holmes, Inc.

ISBN-13: 978-1-945669-69-9

DEDICATION

To the late Linda Jeanne Jones Hart
(The Hobbit)

ACKNOWLEDGMENTS

Thank you for all the help you've given me.

Victoria Lynn Hart Bridwell
Kaitlyn McCoy
Lori Copeland
Barbara Carnegy

CHAPTER ONE

"Aw, shut up!" Joe Brown yelled at his favorite radio station. "I've had enough of your Christmas music." He jabbed viciously at the radio on the dash. "Take that, you old poop." Joe knew nothing about Christmas. He never had a decorated Christmas tree let alone presents under it. Sure, he had seen them in the department store windows and the truck stops he had frequented, but they were not something that he had any background within his family. He remembered his dad's words: *'Joey that crap is not for us. Don't get mixed up with those people, all they want is your money.'* He didn't know much about diesel engines either, but he sure knew when one was not working right. It was screaming for repair and piercing his ears.

It didn't help that snow was coming down in

blizzard form and accumulating faster on the windshield than swishing wipers were able to remove. His vision impaired, by an almost white out and the diesel engines malfunction, made Joe's nerves taut. The big rig was barely moving East on interstate 44 and was surging in buckled jumps. He was afraid to pull to the shoulder and get out for fear he would get stuck. Joe didn't know enough about what was under the hood of an eighteen wheeler to identify the trouble.

The truck bucked on. Automobiles were flying past and some were honking their horns. Joe stuck his hand out his side window and raised his middle finger to the honkers. "Yeah, I hate you too." He yelled. In frustration he felt like crying, but he was not one to cry so he just swallowed hard. With relief, Joe came to an exit and guided the big rig up the ramp with skill. As he crossed over the overpass his eyes focused on the right side of the road looking for a sign he knew to be there.

There it is, he thought. He pressed his brake hard to slow and then realized the almost snow covered sign was not the one he was looking for. Joe pressed the accelerator and the engine screamed even louder as it started forward again. The sign had read: **Heart and soul repair.** An arrow pointed to the right. Through his right window he could barely make out the visage of a small lighted building with a steeple on top.

"A church." He grumbled in disgust. Joe knew nothing about churches either. Only what his dad had told him. *'Joey, stay away from those places, they only want your money.'*

In irritation Joe let the truck bump on down the road, watching closely. There was the sign he had been searching for: **Truck and trailer repair.** An arrow pointed to the left. "Humph." He grunted. The two signs struck him as funny and he laughed out loud. The motor rumbled louder as he turned the limping truck onto the garage lot of the big truck stop.

"Come on, baby, one more hurdle and you'll be able to get yourself back together." Joe talked to the truck like it was human. After all, a truck had been his best friend for ten years.

The only life Joe had ever known was the road. His parents were transient farm workers. They drove an old, blue Ford pick-up following food harvest from place to place. Joe and his younger sister Suzy, by two years, had been in almost every state by his tenth birthday. They had an old tent with a flap down the middle that separated it into two sections. One side was for living and one side for sleeping.

They each had their own thin, sleeping mattress and blanket, kept rolled up when not in use. Their mother, Sally, did her cooking on a small coal oil two burner stove. Everything they owned was packed into a few cardboard boxes and carried under a black plastic, tarp in the back of the pick-up.

Faded, green, triangle shaped canvass and wood camp stools, their only chairs. If there were no showers available Sally had to heat water, from a common well available to workers, for bathing and cooking. Clothing was washed in a small tub, also sometimes used for bathing, or any creek they might come across in their travels. The clothes were then draped over the sides of the truck to dry. Ironed clothing never crossed their backs. When weather turned off cool the children were sent into a nearby forest to collect wood to build a campfire to keep warm. Existing was a constant struggle.

Bob, having had an eighth grade education, was in charge of teaching the children. He was very diligent when it came to what he called, '*the book work*'. Every evening for one hour he worked with Joe and Suzy; he had taught them to read, write and do math. He insisted on them reading any book they got their hands on, which were few. Sometimes in the winter they were enrolled in a school for periods of short duration, but in no time they moved on and maybe there would be another school.

They never were in a school long enough to make friends. No one in the schools they attended wanted to get acquainted with the poor shabby kids from the farm workers and the other children who worked the farms were always too busy or tired to be social. Bob and Sally were never able to get ahead, because Bob always managed to find a bar on payday. He was difficult to get along with for several days after. Life was hard times.

When Joe turned sixteen he ran off and joined a traveling circus. After being with them for two years he got his CDL license and started driving a huge truck full of equipment. His only regret in going was leaving Suzy behind. He had whispered to her as he packed his few articles of clothing into a plastic bag that he would try to make enough money to come back and take her away too. Suzy had cried and begged him not to leave, but he sneaked out of the tent in the early morning hours anyway. He did not look back.

Three years later he came across his folks in California. They were filling their old truck up with gas at the truck stop where he had stopped to eat. He discovered Suzy had run off and married a Marine she met at a county fair. The parents had heard from her and she had informed them she was happy and would be living in San Diego. She had no regrets or hard feelings and asked them to visit her sometime when they came through that area. She had said she loved them, just couldn't live their way any longer.

"I know what she means, Pa. I hope you and Ma don't hold it against us for leaving."

"No, son." Bob's hands were shaking and his voice cracked. "We always knew it would come sometime. Didn't we Ma?" Sally shook her head, yes. They all had tears in their eyes and clung to each other. Joe took them into the restaurant and bought their dinner. They gave him Suzy's address and he gave them a box address and telephone number to reach him in emergencies.

"Can you spare a few dollars, son?" Bob ask as Joe was climbing into the cab of his truck. "You know I hate to ask you, but work has been a little slow for us lately and we don't move as fast as we used to. It don't come in like before when you and Suzy helped us. He wanted to instill guilt. "We're having hard times." Bob had noticed the bills in Joe's wallet when he paid the check to the waitress.

He had also noticed how much the tip was that Joe left.

"Oh yeah, Pa, I'm glad you reminded me." Joe said as he slid back out of the truck. "I meant to give you and Ma some cash." He pulled out his billfold and took out two fifty dollar bills. "I'm giving this to Ma, because I know what you do with a little dough." He looked seriously into his dad's eyes.

"It's, okay, honey," Sally said. "Pa gave up the bottle when you kids left. He thought his drinking was what made you both want to leave."

"Now, Ma, let's don't go into all that now, Joey don't want to hear it. But, son," Bob looked with tears and pain in his eyes at Joe. "I sure hope you both don't hate me."

"How could we hate you?" Joe pulled them both into a hug. "Who taught us how to read and write and do our math? You two taught us how to be hard workers; how to get by in life and to survive. You gave us life." He kissed them both. "Don't ever think we don't love you. You mean more to us than anyone in the world."

"Oh, I hope so," Sally said. She kissed his hand as he crawled back into the cab. "I miss you so much; hope we see you again soon."

"You will, Ma, I'll always be able to find you," he laughed, "I know your route. You can't get rid of me that easy, now that I've found you. Now, I gave you my address and a telephone number, if you need me, call. Joe looked into his side mirror as he pulled onto the highway; they stood beside their old truck, two old people, hand in hand; with tears in his eyes, he watched 'til they disappeared. He felt uncomfortable and didn't know why. Sadness filled his heart and he wanted to run back and cling to them again and find that little boy they raised, and experience those protective hands on him, but he kept on moving down the road. It had hurt him to see the age in their faces and he knew it wouldn't be much longer until they would have to give up the life they led. He knew no matter how they had lived he loved them and they loved him and Suzy. They had done the best they could.

Joe went to San Diego a year later when the Circus disbanded and he found himself out of a job. Suzy was pregnant, but very happy with Edward Smith, her new husband. He found he liked his brother-in-law and could see he treated his Suzy well. He spent a few days there and left them happy and waiting for the coming baby. He promised to visit again every time he came through. He had signed on with a freight trucking company.

Six months later Joe got to hold their new baby and it affected him in a way he didn't understand. He touched the baby's hair, soft skin and marveled at his small features. He saw his parents, Suzy and even himself in the little face. It made Joe tear up, when the wiggling bundle looked up and he saw his own blue eyes looking back intently at him. Little Eddie smiled and gurgled at Joe when he touched his cheek. It was love at first sight. He had never held a baby and a deep affinity set in Joe's heart that day. It put in motion a longing in him that caused an unidentifiable desire.

"Little Eddie definitely has his Uncle Joe's blue

eyes and my blond hair," Suzy commented, smiling at Joe with pride. She ruffled Joe's dark curly hair and teased him with kisses on his cheeks.

"Ah...Suzy, someone's watching." They both laughed, that was a line Joe had always touted to her growing up when she would try to kiss him while he tried to out run her. It was their old game.

Joe stayed two days and didn't want to leave when his load was ready. He had felt comfortable and almost a part of their small family. In the past, the disdain he felt for the hard life he endured growing up soured him on even the thought of marriage or family. Joe never let those foreign thoughts enter his mind often; that was not for him. When he left he assured Suzy he would be back soon.

When the circus he worked for had shut down, Joe had gotten a job with a large trucking company that moved goods from factories to retail stores. His route was mostly in the mid-west and southern states. All his mail came to him through his home base at the broker's office. It made him happy when he got a letter and learned Big Ed would be stationed in North Carolina. He loaded furniture there often and trucked it to Missouri, Oklahoma and Arkansas. He checked in often to his base.

Joe's needs were few; so he did not spend much money and saved most of his earnings. He came across his parents occasionally and always gave them money. He was happy to be able to do it. The truck had a convenient sleeping compartment and he had purchased a small ice box to carry a few bottles of water and snacks. He ate two meals a day in truck stops along the way. He knew all the places that had the best breakfast and dinners. Every evening, when he stopped at a truck stop for the night, he would walk, run, and exercise to stay in shape.

Joe rarely got time off, but when he did and could not locate his parents or be close to Suzy, the baby, and Ed, he would check into a cheap motel and spend a few days meandering through the town he was in. He often walked through parks, fed the birds and would observe families laughing and playing together. His thoughts always wandered to Suzy and her little family.

The feelings he experienced pierced a place inside him that made him lonely and longing for something he could not name. He would watch and smile and laugh seeing the strangers enjoying each other. Sometimes he would strike up conversation with families he encountered, and they would let him share a few minutes of joy with them. The few acquaintances he acquired were waitresses, other truckers or attendants in truck stations.

A real family life was a dream he hid in the far corners of his mind; only to be brought out to think about when he lay alone in his sleeper during idle time. The dream was always illusive.

CHAPTER TWO

Joe was startled by a man pecking on his window and quickly rolled the glass down. He presumed this man was a mechanic there to tell him where to park.

"You're a sight for sore eyes." Joe exclaimed rolling the window down. "This girl has something powerfully wrong with the engine. Where do you want me?"

"Well…" the attendant drawled, "You can park anywhere you want. I hate to tell you this, but the garage is closed until after Christmas. I just locked the door."

"What?" Joe cried in alarm. "It can't be. I've got to be in Springfield by Monday morning. There's no way unless I get a mechanic."

"Sorry, bud. This is Christmas Eve. There is no one here and I only work in the office. I've got some little kids waiting for Santa." He gestured to a running car where Joe could see two little faces pressed against the back window and a woman in the front seat looking inquisitively out at his rig. "Even the restaurant is closed. If you're hungry, I suggest you go across the street to the church. They've got food and it's free to anyone who wants it."

The man turned and quickly ran toward his vehicle. Joe saw the children jumping up and down and getting very excited when their dad got in and closed his door. The wife scooted close, then reached up and kissed her husband's lips. Red tail lights blurred in the falling snow as the man pulled his car onto the high way.

"I'm not going over to that church," Joe huffed. "I'll bet it's free." He felt angry and somehow betrayed. He had never known a truck stop to be closed. He felt helpless and hopeless. He remembered the last TA truck stop he had passed; the lot had been loaded with trucks. It just became apparent to him this lot was empty, except for a few old empty discarded trailers and a disabled cab or two. There must have been a message put up somewhere and he had missed it. He was still sulking and peeved with himself; even though he knew if he had been able to stop at the other place he would have done so. He slapped his hand against the steering wheel. "Why didn't you mess up sooner if you were going to?" If he had owned a cat he would have kicked it too. He was very frustrated.

I don't believe this, Joe kept thinking. He knew this stop to have a small diner, but to be closed just because it is Christmas Eve irritated him.

What's so special about Christmas, he thought. Then another thought came rudely into his mind. Realization that he had forgotten to asked the man if they would be closed on Christmas Day.

"Drat, I bet they are," he grumbled.

Joe parked the truck in an empty spot near the work barn. He wanted to be the first one in when someone showed up to work. His cab was getting colder all the time and his fuel was getting lower. He didn't think it would be sensible to run the motor for heat, especially since the motor was still making such a racket.

So, he crawled into the sleeping compartment, pounded the lumpy pillow, covered with an old blanket and lay his head down. He soon dozed off to sleep until cold and hunger woke him. Joe's stomach began to rumble to remind him it was empty. Dusk was upon him and he was growing hungrier and colder. He'd had no lunch and his only prospect for food was across the road. His mother's words about churches came to mind. *'Joey, good people go to church and they think God was made only for them, not for the likes of us. It just ain't for our kind.'*

Joe had wanted to ask her, "*What kind are we?*" But he never did, because her words sounded so final he was afraid to hear the answer. He had never given himself much thought, except to know he was born to work. Sally had taught her children they had to be clean and tidy, but they were never to think too highly of themselves. After all, they were just migrant workers and owned nothing, but the old truck and the thrift store clothes on their backs.

When Joe had gotten out on his own and earned money, he had begun to buy clothes in a western or farm store; not a thrift store. He would never forget how embarrassed and ignorant he felt the day he asked one of the other drivers where he bought his clothes. He walked humbly into that store and was surprised at the choices he saw. He walked in feeling ill at ease and walked out feeling like a regular guy. No one in the place treated him any different than the next one in line to pay. He loved Levi's, western shirts and soft leather, cowboy boots on his feet. They made him feel kind of normal. He washed his laundry at big truck stops where he took showers.

CHAPTER THREE

Joe's growling hungry stomach forced him to come
to grips with his fear of churches and the good
people who go there. He locked his truck, bundled
up in coveralls, hat and gloves; then struggled
through the snow to cross the road. Someone was
clearing the parking lot of the church, but the new
snow was covering it up faster than the blade could
remove it. The driver inside the enclosed tractor cab
gave Joe a wave and a hearty smile. Joe waved and
smiled back.

Joe felt like a bum begging, and hung back as he
watched a group of people come out the side door
of a building attached to the church. His people
were always poor, but never had to beg; he was
uncomfortable. The light over the door was warm
and welcoming and he could see others inside

sitting at tables before the door closed to. They seemed to be eating, laughing and having a good time. Another man came out the door and followed those leaving to their car. He was wishing, "Merry Christmas," hugging them and shaking their hands. As he turned to go back inside he noticed Joe.

"Hello, young man. I'm Pastor Bill." The man walked straight up to, Joe. "Can I help you with something?" He stuck out his hand to shake Joe's large palm.

"Ah…" Joe shuffled his feet and did not look the pastor in the eye. He's going to throw me out now, he thought. "A man over at the truck stop told me to come over here." He blurted out, as thought it was someone else's fault he was there. "The restaurant is closed over there. He said I could get something to eat here." Joe finally looked up. "I'm not a beggar," he assured, "I can pay for what I eat. It's just that there is no place else." He added demurely.

"Come on in." Bill took Joe by the arm with gusto and guided him through the side door into a warm, large room scattered with tables where others were laughing, talking and eating. "As you can see we've got quite a crowd," he chortled and gestured to the room, "and there's not a beggar among them."

Joe looked sharply into Bill's face and saw the teasing, laughter in the minister's eyes. He snickered and began to exhale the breath he had been holding and relaxed. He introduced himself and told Bill of his position.

"Well…," the pastor said thoughtfully, "I can help with the food, but I don't know anyone except the boy's across the street who repair diesel truck motors and as you said they are on holiday. You must have seen our sign out front, it reads: **Heart and Soul repair.** The sign on their side reads: **Truck and Trailer repair.** He clapped his hands together. "Get a plate and fill it up," he injected enthusiastically. "We do have plenty of food. Thanks, to the good ladies in the kitchen. I'll try to keep you busy 'til the boy's return in a few days."

Joe's mind picked up on, '*the good ladies'*, and his stomach did a little flip flop. When he went through the food line those ladies filled his plate to overflowing and were generous with smiles and welcoming comments. He was amazed.

Joe could not remember ever having eaten such a good meal as he shoved the last bites of a homemade dinner roll into his mouth. He was warm and comfortable and his stomach was full. He felt contented and sleepy.

Pastor Bill was beckoning him from a door into the sanctuary. Just as the others did Joe left his plate for the ladies who were cleaning off the tables and ambled over to the preacher.

"We're getting ready to start our Christmas service. I hope you'll join us. I believe you'll enjoy it. Our children's choir has worked really hard on the presentation of this play."

"Sure," Joe said. After all, it was the least he could do in appreciation for the dinner. He followed Bill in and saw the room was almost full, but Joe finally found a seat on the end half-way down the aisle. He gazed around and observed the simplicity of the room. The wood floors shinned like they had just been polished and were squeaky clean. Simple red drapes hung over long windows along one side. The benches were cushioned covered and comfortable to sit on. An older piano was barely able to be seen behind all the poinsettia's piled on and around it. There were some large, painted scene boards strung around the stage and young men were beginning to move them around in order for the play. The room darkened and everyone who had been talking became quiet.

Recorded music began to play softly. Some children dressed as angels rushed out of a door on the side of the stage acting very excited, soft light beamed onto them. They lined up in an arc around the back of a podium in front of a screen painted like a cloudy sky.

Lights came on and the music stopped. A girl came forward and announced, "This is, the Christmas Story according to Luke." She began to read words from a book laid there about a baby who was born in a barn, to a virgin, named Mary. He was wrapped in swaddling clothes, laid in a manger and named Jesus. The lights were dimmed and children began to sing, *'Away in a Manger.'*

Rustling sound was being heard in the far, right corner of the stage. A bright spot light shined brightly over a screen painted like a barn on that side of the stage. A teenage girl, identified in the reading as Mary, sat in a wooden hut beside a small basket. Bundles of straw were stacked all around. She reached over and patted a baby doll. A papier-mâché donkey and cow lay around the basket and a boy, identified in the story as Joseph, stood over her. They were dressed in long robes. The bright light darkened and the children's choir began to sing '*Ole little town of Bethlehem,*' in a gentle quite voice. A small star like light stayed on above the hut.

The girl at the podium returned to the others and one of the older boys came forth, took the book and read of angels coming from heaven to speak to shepherds who were in the fields watching over their sheep. The bright light again focused on a country scene to the left. A girl and a boy angel came rushing out of the group into a spot light and spoke to two boys dressed as shepherds. The shepherds ducked as though they were afraid.

"Fear not, we bring good tidings." said the girl angel.

"Today, a savior has been born to you. He is Christ the Lord," said the boy angel. They returned to their place in the angel group.

The choir began to sing, '*Hark the herald Angel's Sing.*' Suddenly all the angel group rushed to the manger scene and shouted in unison: "Glory to God in the highest and on earth peace good will to men." They angels returned to their original places.

The two shepherds gathered their staffs and the bright light followed them over to the manger scene. The shepherds bowed to the baby and sat down to observe the babe. The choir sang *Joy to the World".*

Then, three, beautifully dressed boys, with crowns on their heads, came onto the stage, bowed and lay gifts in front of the babe. The angel choir sang: "*We three kings'*.

All the actors gathered together and sang, "*O Come all ye Faithful'.* The play ended when a boy came forward and announced: "This same babe that was born that first Christmas morning grew to be a man and was crucified for all our sins on a cross. He rose from the grave and became the Savior of all men. He went back to his father in heaven, but has promised to return again. We are waiting for Him to this day." The whole cast took a bow individually. The audience applauded and gave the players a standing ovation.

Pastor Bill took the stage clapping and grinning. "Give them another hand." He gestured to the whole stage of happy faces as they filed off the stage.

The Pastor gave a short talk about the man the baby became and how He was a Gift from God. He asked everyone to remember God's most precious Gift when they celebrated their holiday at home. The celebration of His birth each year stood to remind everyone of the hope He brought to the World.

"Where would we be without our blessed Savior, Jesus?" Bill asked. "God gave His Son to die on the cross for us and He shed His blood to cover our sins for salvation. Let us all go to our homes with gratitude for the Gift He gave us and remember to keep Christmas in our hearts all year. Merry, Christmas all." The service ended with a prayer from one of the church deacons.

CHAPTER FOUR

Joe did not understand everything the minister was talking about, but noticed everyone else seemed to. They were shaking their heads and saying, "Amen." The congregation stood up and hugged and shook hands and commented on the play and how the choir had done such a good job. All those who noticed Joe walked up to him, shook his hand or hugged him and wished him, "Happy Holiday or Merry Christmas." He smiled and nodded. Beautiful story, if only the story was true, he thought.

When Joe went back into the dining room to collect his coveralls and cap; he noticed Bill getting his hat and coat too. He walked over to the man.

"I want to thank you preacher. You were right. That play was wonderful. I don't believe I have ever enjoyed anything so much. I wish there was something I could do to repay you for all your kindness."

"Do you really mean that, Joe?" Bill asked in excitement.

"I sure do, just you name it," Joe said. He did not know you do not tell a preacher you'll do anything for him, because he'll find you a job. He followed Bill out the door into the cold still night. The snow was no longer falling and it looked almost as bright as day.

The sky was clear and the stars were blinking brightly in the dark night sky. The star over the manger in the play came into his mind. He stared up in wonder and was overwhelmed with the feeling that there was a power up there he had not known before. He felt like a speck in relation to this physical force, but he was not afraid. He knew peace.

"Joe, you see that big barn where the yard light is on at that big white house over there." Bill pointed off about a city block distance to the North. "A widow who attends our church lives there and is unable to feed her cattle. She's been ill and I told her I would do it for her, but I really need to get home. I have company from out of state waiting for me. You know how that is."

Joe shook his head, even though he had not a clue about company from out of town. He had never had company. His idea of company was arriving at a new work farm and seeing a familiar face he recognized.

"I can drop you at her lane. It will only take a few minutes to go to the barn and throw out some hay for the animals; it's only a short walk back here." The preacher gestured toward the church. "You come back to the side door over there; it will be open. Stay the night here. There are others staying the night too and it'll be warmer than your sleeper. The workers are taking down tables, putting up cots and laying out quilts as we speak."

"Sure, I can do that," Joe said. He was happy to think of a warm place to sleep after having gotten so cold earlier.

"I'll call Mrs. Johnson right now so she'll be expecting you." Bill took out his cell telephone and began dialing. It was evident he was pleased to be relieved of the job.

Joe trudged through the snow up the widow's lane. He went past the house, through a gate, on into the barn yard and let himself into the building. A bare light bulb lit up the barn. He inhaled the fragrance of horses, cattle, feed and hey. The smell was not offensive to his nose; he liked the odors that blended to a normal barn scent.

Two horses in separate stalls snorted at him, stomped their hoofs and raised their ears. He served them some of the hay he found there and they seemed satisfied, but still watched him warily with big bright eyes. A big yellow cat jumped from the loft onto a stack of square bales and startled Joe. For a few seconds they gazed into each other's eyes. Joe reached out to pet the cat and it raced out of the barn. He chuckled to himself to see the fear in the cat's eyes.

"I'll not hurt you, kitty," he said to the departing feline.

There sat a green tractor already loaded with a huge bale of hay in its bucket. The machine started right up. Using the tractor reminded him of the circus when he fed the animals. Joe drove out into a field where a large herd of black cattle came bawling and following after. He dropped the bucket and the hay bale rolled off in a loud thud. He descended the tractor and removed the netting from the bale and began to break up the tightly packed hay. The cattle eyed him warily at first then moved in and began to eat; keeping an eye on him.

"It's alright, babies, I won't hurt you." Joe soothed. A cow turned and looked intently at this stranger, but she didn't leave her place. She uttered a low sound and a calf hunkered close to her side and began to nurse. Joe smiled as he watched the cattle. He could feel the heat from their bodies and see the mist from their breath. It warmed his heart to see these simple animals. He had never been this close to cattle before. His only experience with this kind of animal's were the cattle trucks he had seen on truck stop lots. They are beautiful, he thought. He closed the gate as he left the pasture.

Joe parked the tractor back in the barn where he had found it. The horses allowed him to touch their soft velvety noses. They each wanted his attention. While stroking their silky coat he noticed their water tanks were almost empty. He searched and found a water hydrant inside the barn with a bucket nearby. He refilled their tanks and said. "That ought to keep you two 'til morning." A smile came on his face and it warmed his heart. He shut the barn up tight to help keep the horses warm.

"Are you, Joe?" A feminine voice called from the porch as he passed the house.

"Sure am," Joe answered. He stepped on the porch and removed his cap.

"Come on in for some hot cocoa." A young woman invited, opening the door. "It's terribly cold out there."

"Oh, you don't need to go to any trouble for me." She just waved him inside. Joe stepped shyly in and she shut the door firmly behind him.

"You can't possibly know how much I appreciate your help. Brother Bill called and told me of the trouble with your truck." She gave him a sorrowful look. "I'm so sorry for you. What a time for this to happen." She pointed to an overstuffed chair. "Have a seat and I'll get you some hot cocoa. The boys and I were just getting settled in for some before their bedtime." She moved out of the room.

Joe looked around the warm cozy room with a fire in the fireplace. The burning wood odor was pleasant to his senses. What a comfortable place he thought. He had rarely been in private homes before. He wondered if she was the widow, then noticed a picture of a young soldier man on the mantle and decided she was the widow. There seems to be a lot of young widows these days, he thought.

On the sofa sat a small boy and beside him a baby tightly wrapped in a blue blanket was propped on a pillow. The boy smiled sheepishly at the stranger. They both stared calmly at Joe.

"Hi,' Joe said and grinned shyly at the older child.

The boy jumped off the sofa and came right over to Joe. "You want to hold the new baby?" he asked.

"Ah…I don't know." Joe was uneasy. The only baby he had ever held was Suzy's baby, Eddie.

"You can. Mama says he won't break."

"Well…maybe I shouldn't."

"Timmy," the woman entered the room carrying a try of steaming cups, "Leave Joe alone. Not everyone wants to hold Davy." She handed a cup to Joe. "He's so proud of his new brother. He thinks everyone wants to hold him." She sat a cup on a table for the boy. "Drink up. It's about time for your bed."

Joe hastily drank the chocolate, for he felt out of place. "Thank you, Mrs. Johnson." he stood up quickly. "That sure hit the spot. I've got to leave now, but don't you worry, I'll be back in the morning to feed the cattle and horses." He was backing out the door as he spoke.

CHAPTER FIVE

Next morning, Joe folded up the cot and blanket he had used the night before. It had felt good to lie in a bed that was not in the cab of a truck, even if it was just a cot. He had hurried to Mrs. Johnson's earlier, before any of the others sleepers had awaken and gone to her barn, fed the horses the small bales stacked there and loaded hey on the tractor from huge bales packed beside the barn and carried some out to the cattle.

When he had arrived back at the church he was met with the smell of hickory smoked bacon, scrambled eggs, biscuits and gravy, hash browned potatoes, and lots of hot coffee. His stomach growled with the want of the food. Afterward, he tried to pay one of the ladies and she refused.

"How about I give you a tip then?"

"Oh no," the pretty red headed woman said. "This is a blessing for me to be able to serve you. I could never take money." She laughed at Joe's exasperated frown. "You just need to learn to accept a gift, young man. You owe nothing, Merry Christmas." She walked away smiling.

Joe reached onto a counter beside the coffee machine for a tooth pick when he felt a large hand on his back. He turned around and saw it was Pastor Bill.

"Joe, you must have done a good job at Mrs. Johnson's and were back there feeding this morning You're a good man to have around; we may never let you leave." The minister laughed. "I told you I would keep you busy 'til your trucks fixed. Katy called and has asked that you come over to her house for dinner, right after church that is." Bill grinned. "We don't want you to miss this morning's service. It's Christmas you know. We have to celebrate the Lord's birthday."

"Sure, sure," said Joe."I'll be there, but she don't owe me a dinner." He was thinking of the discomfort he had felt at Mrs. Johnsons the night before.

The Pastor told Joe how David Johnson had gone off to Iraq, not knowing his wife was expecting a second child. He had been there only a few months when he walked into a mine and was killed instantly.

"She's quite a brave woman. She's been taking care of that farm alone until she had that baby about six weeks ago. We tried to give her help before, but she refused our offer. Said David, would want her to take care of things the way he liked it done. I'd appreciate it Joe if you could help her out until they get your truck going. Please stay here at night until your truck is fixed. Someone is always here to see to our quest"

"Why…I have nothing else to do. I kind of like being around all those animals. Except that cat, I think she hates me."

"That cats a tom and he probably does hate you if you called him a she." Bill smiled. "Don't worry though, when he wants to, he'll warm to you and then he won't let you alone."

"Mrs. Katy Johnson won't have to cook for me. I'm happy to be able to be of use to someone and it gives me something to do. No, she doesn't owe me a dinner." Joe was glad to hear Mrs. Johnson's first name. She looked more like a Katy than a Mrs. Johnson.

"Joe, let the woman show her appreciation in the best way she knows how; besides you ain't tasted her cooking." Pastor Bill turned his lips into a big smile. "She's gooood."

CHAPTER SIX

The songs sung by the adult choir were beautiful and brought joy to Joe's soul. He sang from the hymnal with the rest of the congregation and felt at ease with himself. His deep voice blended with all the others. He had never sung with a group of people before. His singing had amounted to singing along with the country music station on his radio. He looked around and saw smiles, love and contentment on the faces of those close to him. After Pastor Bill said a prayer everyone shook hands or hugged the people closest to them. Then…they sang some more songs.

Mama, Joe thought, *you misjudged these church people. I don't see a one who acts like he thinks he is better than anyone else.*

Pastor Bill began his sermon commenting on the

baby who grew into the man, Jesus Christ. He told how He had endured temptation and overcame. He told how He was crucified on a cross to save mankind from sin. He was very graphic about what Jesus suffered. How he would come again someday and give everlasting life to every man, woman and child who believe he died for their sin; rose from the grave and accepted him as their Savior.

He addressed man's sin and how he needed to repent and turn his life away from this sin. He talked about what sin was and how you must admit your sin. How each person is separated from God because of his sin; *"For all have sin and fall short of the Glory of God."* (Rom. 3:23). Bill read from the same book the children had read the story of Luke. You must admit your sins to God and ask for His forgiveness. *"For the wages of sin is death, but the gift of God is eternal life."* (Rom. 6:23).

Sin! Something Joe had never given thought to. No one had ever talked to him about personal sin or any kind of sin. He wasn't even sure what it was, but it sure made him feel uncomfortable to hear Bill talk about its consequences.

"If you confess with your mouth, 'Jesus is Lord,' and believe in your heart that God raised him from the dead, you will be saved. For it is with your heart that you believe and are justified, and it is with your mouth that you confess, and are saved." (Rom. 10:9-10) Pastor Bill read these words from the book he held in his hand.

"It's your choice," he said. Would you like to make that choice today? Is God leading you?"

The choir and congregation began to sing,

"Amazing grace! How sweet the sound. That saved a wretch like me! I once was lost, but now am found, was blind, but now I see."

"You can be free from sin today," Pastor Bill was saying. "It's your choice. All you have to do is accept Jesus as your Savior: believe in Him, repent and be baptized in His name." Bill invited all who wanted to be rid of their sin to come to the altar and pray to God and ask forgiveness. "I'll pray with you." he said, "others are praying for you now. Come and accept His Gift and become one of His children today. '*For God so loved the world that He gave His one and only Son, that whoever believes in Him shall not parish, but have everlasting life."* (John 3:16)

I don't know how to pray, Joe thought. He knew he wanted that Gift of God's, but he was afraid to go down to the altar in front of all these people he did not know; and confess *WHAT?* …he did not know. He did identify with some of the sin the preacher mentioned and knew he was guilty.

The choir was singing, *"My chains are gone, I've been set free. My God, my savior has ransomed me."*

"Oh, God," Joe whispered. "I know I'm not worth much, but show me the way. I want to be free." How, he thought, could they have done what they did to you? It brought him mental anguish.

His body shaking and tears on his face, he stumbled down the aisle. He felt something powerful leading him and he told Pastor Bill. "I want God's greatest Gift. I want His Son, Jesus, as my Savior."

Bill took Joe into his arms and motioned for some of his deacons to join him. He guided him to the altar and they knelt down with him. Each of the men put their hands on Joe and Pastor Bill began to pray. "Thank you, Lord, for sending Joe to us. He wants to become one of your children. His heart is heavy and he wants your forgiveness."

"Oh, yes," Joe spoke softly. He was astonished as each man prayed with him at the change he felt overcome himself; like a dam had burst within and let go of all the emotional pain he carried inside for so long. He felt enveloped in the warmth of the Holy Spirit and a smile came on his face. His tears were dried and he was filled with a joy he had never known.

"Thank you, God. You didn't really need me, but you knew I needed you. Thank you. Thank you," Joe prayed aloud.

Each Deacon hugged Joe and smiled at him with love. He felt like he already knew each one of them and did not even know their names,

Bill hugged Joe hard and welcomed him into the family of God. "I told you, Joe," he smiled broadly, "we do, **HEART AND SOUL REPAIR,** here."

CHAPTER SEVEN

Joe had freshened up inside the men's toilet and fetched a clean shirt from his truck to put on before he left the church annex building. When he showed at Kate Johnson's door for dinner, he felt really free and clean inside. He was a new person, not just truck driver Joe, but someone who really mattered.

Timmy opened the door to Joe's soft knock "Come on in, Joe, you can sit over there." He pointed to the big recliner by the fireplace where Joe had set the night before. "She's almost got it ready. Mama," he called loudly, "Joe's here."

"Sit, Joe. It's almost ready. Just taking the Chicken out of the oven," Kate called from the next room.

"Thank you, Timmy. Where's Davy?" Joe asked.

"Oh, he's asleep. That's all he ever does. Poop,

cry and sleep. You want to go watch him? I watch him all the time." He motioned with a stuck up thumb towards the kitchen. "She won't care."

"That's alright I'll wait 'til he wakes up," Joe answered. He began to feel a little of the anxiety he had felt the night before and wondered what he was doing in this house. He felt like he was in someone else's place.

"Come on in boys. Joe, you can sit at that end of the table, I've put you a place there."

I have never seen anything so pretty, Joe thought as he looked at her table. Kate had place mats, candles, real silver ware, and there were so many pieces he wasn't sure which piece to use first. He had never sat at a table set like this before; it made him uneasy.

"Joe, would you like to say the prayer or do you want me to?" Kate reached for his and Timmy's hand.

"That's okay, you do it," Joe said. He had never prayed over a meal before. In fact his first prayers had been this very morning when he ask God to save him. Her prayer was simple and thankful to God for blessings, food, and finally for Joe's help. He suddenly realized he had so much to learn about being a Christian.

She passed each bowl to Joe in turn and started conversation with so much ease, that in just a few minutes into the meal he began to relax and enjoy all the beautiful food and sweet tea. He watched her put her napkin on her lap and pick up a fork: he did the same. As she talked she smiled and laughed at her own stories of farm life. Joe could hardly take his eyes from her face. She also, told how she and David had taken his father's farm over after he had died. David's mother had passed many years before. "We worked hard." A sad look came on her face and small tears of emotion gathered in the corner of her eyes.

"We were just two young kids and yet we made this place into a profitable farm. Timmy was just a baby. Then David decided he should do his duty and join the Army. He had never gone anywhere before and one of his friends went and wrote how great it was. All of a sudden he had wonder lust. We didn't know I was pregnant at the time, in fact, he never knew before…" Her voice became a whisper. "I don't know what he was thinking; that I could run this place without him." She got quiet and lowered her head.

Her light brown hair lay curled softly around her ears and her dark brown eyes seemed to penetrate right inside Joe's being. Her cheeks had a slight blush from the heat of her cooking and her trembling lips were barely colored. He found himself wanting to kiss those lips, take her in his arms and comfort her.

He felt his own face get heated. He wanted to take away the pain he saw on her face. He knew she couldn't read his thoughts, but he still felt embarrassed by them. He felt he had somehow violated her, because of what he was thinking; he had no right to touch her. He was finally able to pull his eyes away from her and look at the table. She regained her composure and said. "Oh, I should not be going on like this." She smiled and let out a deep sigh. "I hope you liked the meal," she said.

The dinner was all Pastor Bill said it would be and more. He regretted when it was over and asked if he could help her clean up.

"No, no, let's take our coffee into the living room and I'll clean all this up later. There's no need to hurry to clean up." She jumped up and went into the kitchen to get the coffee. "Christmas is a day to enjoy, not work."

Kate handed him a cup and carried her mug of coffee. He followed her into the other room, with Timmy tailing right behind. She sat her cup on a table in front of the sofa and slid a coaster under his on the small stand beside the recliner she motioned him to. Joe lowered his eyes to the flowered rug on the floor to keep from staring at her.

"Oh," Timmy yelled as a loud wail came from the bedroom. "He's hungry again, Mama."

"Oh dear," Kate said. She looked very flustered. "I'm sorry, Joe. I'll have to go to the bedroom to feed the baby. Will you please excuse me?" She got up and began to move that way.

"Sure, sure, no problem," he said. Discomfort of the night before came over him again. She's in there breast feeding that baby, he thought. What am I doing here? "Maybe I should just go on," Joe called to her.

"Mama, can me and Joe go out and build a snowman?" Timmy yelled to her before she could answer Joe. "It ain't too cold. Sun's shinning and I want to use my new Christmas sled too."

"Well, Timmy, that would be up to Joe." She called from the bedroom. She was hoping Joe would say yes. Timmy had few male figures in his life to give him attention since his father's death.

"Sure I'd like that." Joe drank down his coffee fast and began to put his coverall's on. He couldn't get out of the house fast enough.

"Timmy, be sure to get your warm coat on, your rubber boots and your hat and gloves. The sun may be shinning, but it's still cold out there."

"Yahoo," Timmy yelled and ran to a closet in the hall and began to pull out his belongings. In nothing flat he was dressed for outdoors. He appeared before Joe in the living room with a big smile on his face. "This is gonna' be fun, Joe. I love making a snowman. I used to do it all the time with my daddy. Then, you can pull me on my sled."

CHAPTER EIGHT

As soon as Joe left the porch he was hit in the chest with a wet snowball. He chased the boy down, pulled him to the ground and rubbed a little snow in his face. Timmy fought back and before long they were both wet from rolling in the cold snow. The steam of their breath warmed their noses as they laughed and played. Joe had never played with a small child before and he had to hustle to keep up with Timmy. He slipped from his grasp like a slippery eel. Joe was breathing hard and begged Timmy to rest.

"Hey!" Timmy said, "Let's make some snow angles. I can make snow angels."

"Snow angels?" Joe looked puzzled. "What are snow angels?"

Timmy got up from where he was resting on the

ground and walked to an area where the snow was smooth and had not been molested in their play. He flopped down and began to swish his arms and legs back and forth. Joe got up and watched. Timmy reached his hand up and Joe pulled him out of the snow.

"Look, can you see the angel?" Timmy asked.

"Yes, I can see it." Joe was amazed, turned and smiled down at Timmy, who looked back with true joy on his face

"I told you I could make angels. I can make snowmen too. Let's do it." He started by making a small ball and then began to roll it on the snow one way then another until the snow began to take the shape of a big ball. "Come on, Joe, you make a ball too."

Timmy told Joe how to assemble the three balls they had put together after he had struggled to put the second one on and realized it was too heavy. "Be sure to put the little one on top." Timmy instructed. "It's his head."

Joe patiently followed his instruction, acting as though he knew nothing about making a snowman. "I've never seen such a handsome snow man before, Timmy. You did a really good job." He could see Timmy felt smart and really good about his snowman.

"I know, I do this every year when it snows, but he needs something else. He has no arms or face." Timmy complained,

Joe reached into a dead bush, pulled two stiff stalks off and stuck them into the snowman for arms. "That better?" he asked.

"Yeah, but he still needs more."

"Maybe I can help," Sally called from the porch. She came running to them with her arms full of dressing for the snowman. The boy and man grinned at each other and shook their heads. She put a bright red scarf around its neck, an old felt cowboy hat on his round head, a pickle for the nose, little circles of carrots for his mouth, and two big black buttons for his eyes.

"She's always good with this stuff," said Timmy as he danced around the snowman.

Joe joined in and sang softly, *"Frosty the Snowman,"* along with Kate and Timmy.

"Sing loud, Joe," yelled Timmy.

Joe laughed and took hold of their hands and danced around the handsome sculpture too. He sang the song with them, because he knew it well. He had been singing it along with his radio for years, but had never enjoyed it so much.

"Catch me if you can." Timmy had dropped hands with them and started running wildly around the yard. He threw snow balls at them and dared them to hit him. They laughed and ran after him until they were out of breath. The boy could get around in the deep snow better than the adults. He ran out toward the barn, climbed the gate and hid in the rows of big round baled hey. He was giggling so loud they found him easily. Joe grabbed Timmy up into his strong arms and tickled him until he begged to be put down.

"I can out run you, Joe," Timmy yelled as he bolted over the gate into the yard.

"That boy is something," Joe laughingly told

Kate as he locked the gate behind them.

Snow balls came flying the instant they started toward the house. Joe grabbed Kate's hand as they laughed and ran together after the boy when he ran around the house. They conspired to run the opposite direction in order to overcome him and collided at the first corner they rounded. All three landed in a heap with arms and legs flailing in all directions. Timmy was up and running again, but Kate and Joe were left holding onto each other and lay in the snow face to face.

They were laughing until Joe looked into Kate's eyes and felt like taking her into his arms to kiss her. Their smiles faded and a deep look into each other's eyes sobered both faces. The seconds they stared at each other felt like minutes and finally Joe rolled away and gave her a hand up. It was evident some feeling had occurred between them. It was uncomfortable for both of them.

"Hey, come on. The games not over yet," cried Timmy as he slammed into Joe's legs. "Mama, you go in. Me and Joe are playing."

"Hey, the games over for the day, Timmy." Joe knelt down and adjusted the boy's hat. "I need to be going, but I'll see you tomorrow when I come to feed the animals. Then I'll pull you on the sled"

Joe came for the next two days to play with the boy, eat, and feed the cattle for Kate. He held the sweet baby Davy and did not even get upset when he spit up on his shirt. Katy dabbed at the messy shirt and was embarrassed. Joe assured her he would wash. "It's not his fault I was bouncing him too much. Davy's a gooood boy," Joe cooed with his lips to the baby's smiling face. The baby's lips nibbled at Joe's face and felt like kisses; it touched Joe deeply.

He had put off telling them he had been notified this morning that his rig was ready to go. He had become so close to this little family; he felt a real connection and for the first time he could remember he was not excited to hit the road.

"They got my truck fixed, Katy." Joe stood at the door ready to leave. He was still holding baby Davy. "I'll be moving on first thing in the morning. Guess I'll say goodbye to you and the boys tonight," He said sadly. "I've got to tell you I've never tasted such good food in my life. You're the best cook," He complimented her the only way he could think of for letting him be part of her family the past few days. He knew he would never forget them. "Thank you for all you've done." He pressed the baby into her arms.

"Oh no, Joe," Kate cried. "We owe you thanks." She stood close to him and looked deeply into his blue eyes. "We're gonna' miss you. Not just because you helped us, but because we're really fond of you."

"Where are you going, Joe?" Timmy jumped off the sofa and asked angrily. "Why are you leaving us?" He started to cry.

"I don't want to leave either, boy," but I don't know how not to, Joe thought. He knelt down and took the boy onto his knee and hugged him. Timmy clung tight to his neck.

"Joe, my daddy left and he never came back. Say you will Joe." Timmy's face was wet with tears.

"Say you will."

"Oh, Timmy," Katy knelt to hug her son and Joe. There was pain on her face and tears in her eyes. "Joe, I had no idea this would happen, I'm so sorry." They all cried and clung to each other, none wanted to let go. Joe did not know how to comfort the boy, the woman, or himself. These caring feelings were something new to him.

"Joe, do you come this way often?" Katy pulled away and asked.

"About once a week, I'm gonna' work it so I can be through here on Sundays. Brother Bill gave me a Bible and has consented to help me study. I promised him I'd come."

A smile like sunshine came over Katy's face. "Did you hear that, Timmy? Joe will be back through here real often. You can see him at church on Sundays."

"Is that for real, Joe?" The boy brightened. "But, I really want to see you every day."

"I know I would love to see you every day too, but I got a job, Timmy," Joe chuckled. "And my boss says I got to go back to work or lose it. A man's got to work."

"Joe, would it be too much to ask, if you would have Sunday dinners with us?" Katy asked hopefully.

"If you want me here." he smiled broadly. "Wild horses couldn't tear me away. I'll be here."

Katy and the boys stood on the porch and watched as Joe walked down the drive. "See you next Sunday," she yelled. Timmy made a fast dash into the house and watched from the bedroom window as Joe walked all the way to the Truck Stop. He was still there when Joe pulled off the lot thirty minutes later.

When Joe wheeled his big rig off the Truck Stop lot his heart was full. He saw the signs: **Truck and Trailer Repair** and **Heart and Soul Repair,** and he knew he would never forget them. One got him off the road to fix his truck and the other fixed his heart.

Thank you, God, for the gift of your Son and His salvation, he prayed, *for my repair job and a new life. You gave me your greatest gift ever.*

Joe doesn't know it now, but within the year he will become a farmer and have a new family of his own. God's blessings just keep on coming for those who love Him and keep his commands.

ABOUT THE AUTHOR

Shirley lives in the beautiful Ozarks with her Golden Retriever, Maggie. When Shirley lost her beloved husband she began to fulfill her lifelong dream of writing. The Christmas Gift is her first book. Shirley hopes the inspiration found in this story will remind the reader that the birth of Christ renews all hope in man.